D0364789

Stealing Beauty

STEALING BEAUTY

Screenplay by Susan Minot

from a story by Bernardo Bertolucci

Grove Press

NEW YORK

Published simultaneously in Canada
Printed in the United States of America

FIRST EDITION

Library of Congress Cataloging-in-Publication Data

Minot, Susan.
    Stealing beauty / Susan Minot from a story by Bernardo Bertolucci.
— 1st ed.
        p.   cm.
    ISBN 0–8021–3492–0
    I. Bertolucci, Bernardo.   II. Stealing beauty (Motion picture)
III. Title.
PN1997.S672   1996
791.43'72—dc20   96–19178

Design by Laura Hammond Hough

Grove Press
841 Broadway
New York, NY 10003

10 9 8 7 6 5 4 3 2 1

Stealing Beauty

Cast

Lucy Harmon	*Liv Tyler*
Alex Parish	*Jeremy Irons*
Diana Grayson	*Sinead Cusack*
Ian Grayson	*Donal McCann*
M. Guillaume	*Jean Marais*
Miranda Fox	*Rachel Weisz*
Richard Reed	*D. W. Moffett*
Noemi	*Stefania Sandrelli*
Osvaldo Donati	*Ignazio Oliva*
Carlo Lisca	*Carlo Cecchi*
Michele Lisca	*Franscesco Siciliano*
Niccolò Donati	*Roberto Zibetti*
Christopher Fox	*Joseph Fiennes*
Lieutenant	*Leonardo Treviglio*
Daisy Grayson	*Rebecca Valpy*
Chiarella Donati	*Anna Maria Gherardi*
Gregory	*Jason Flemying*

Crew List

Director	*Bernardo Bertolucci*
Producer	*Jeremy Thomas*
Screenplay by	*Susan Minot*
From a story by	*Bernardo Bertolucci*
Production Supervisor	*Mario Cotone*
UGC production representative	*Yves Attal*
Associate Producer	*Chris Auty*
Director of Photography	*Darius Khondji*
Editor	*Pietro Scalia*
Music composed by	*Richard Hartley*
Production Designer	*Gianna Silvestri*
Costumes by	*Louise Stjernsward*
	and Giorgio Armani
Casting by	*Howard Feuer*
	and Celestia Fox

EXTERIOR. SKY. EARLY MORNING.
Filmed in eight-millimeter video. Clouds. The sound of an airplane.

INTERIOR. AIRPLANE. EARLY MORNING.
The camera pulls back: the frame of an airplane window.

Over a seat the camera picks out Lucy Harmon's face asleep near a window. She is a nineteen-year-old American, full-cheeked, ripe like a plum, with messy hair.

She's reading a book about Tuscany.

Suddenly she looks up, feeling someone watching her. The camera hides.

The clouds part to reveal Pisa's Piazza del Duomo with the Campo dei Miracoli, the Leaning Tower, etc.

INTERIOR. PISA AIRPORT. MORNING.
The camera spying on her, LUCY is at the luggage terminal picking up an old army duffel bag held together with string. A customs dog, sniffing, starts toward her. LUCY is concerned. The dog goes past her to a half-sandwich on the floor.

Outside customs, LUCY is looking lost. Series of shots: fragments of men, old and young, passing by, some looking at her.

LUCY at ticket window. LUCY leaving through airport doors.

INTERIOR. TRAIN. DAY.

Still being shot in video, LUCY asleep with legs up on her bags. Close-up: her forehead, her closed eyes, a trickle of saliva at the corner of her mouth, her neck. Her feet: one boot is off.

Train slowing down. Outside the window a sign for Siena. A man's arm appears, waking LUCY. Around his wrist is a bracelet from the Middle East.

MAN WITH CAMERA
(*offscreen*)

Hey, siamo a Siena . . .
[Hey, we're in Siena . . .]

LUCY wakes, looks at the camera, jumps up. She grabs her bags, her boot. Camera still filming through open window to LUCY on platform. She looks up, putting on a boot.

LUCY

What are you doing?

MAN WITH CAMERA
(*offscreen*)

Mi ricordi qualcuno.
[You remind me of someone.]

The train starts to move.

LUCY

What?

MAN WITH CAMERA
(*offscreen*)
I was on the plane with you.

LUCY
Shit.

MAN WITH CAMERA
This is for you.

Filming switches to thirty-five millimeter. A man's hand snaps the cassette from the video camera. From the moving train he tosses the cassette, which bounces off LUCY and disappears between the wheels. After the train pulls out, it is there on the tracks. LUCY steps down and picks it up.

INTERIOR. TAXI. DAY.
LUCY in the backseat. She digs out a pack of cigarettes and lights one. Car swerves at a corner, throwing her.

LUCY smoking at the window, being jostled. Tuscan countryside passing by. She looks at her journal. Overlapping shots of writing with countryside. A picture in her journal: a detail of a fresco by a fourteenth-century Sienese painter, nearly identical to the real landscape.

EXTERIOR. ROAD. DAY.
The house can be seen on a hill, the countryside spreading out around it. The taxi appears in the distance coming up the road.

INTERIOR. TAXI. DAY.
Through the window Villa Grayson flashing behind the leaves.

EXTERIOR. VILLA GRAYSON DRIVEWAY. DAY.
LUCY is holding her bags, confronting the house. The taxi drives off behind her. She walks toward the entrance.

INTERIOR. IAN'S STUDIO. DAY.
LUCY steps into a quiet, dark house. She carries her bag through a studio, a room with wine barrels.

> LUCY
>
> Hello! . . . hello?

In the living room, she puts down her bags and picks a cherry from a bowl. She notices a woman, NOEMI, asleep among some cushions, snoring softly.

EXTERIOR. PERGOLA. GARDEN. DAY.
LUCY steps through the terrace door into a bright, dappled day. An elderly gentleman is asleep with a Panama hat over his face. The lawn is populated with terra-cotta statues, which seem to watch us. She walks to a chaise where a woman sleeps in the shade of a pergola. DIANA GRAYSON is a handsome Englishwoman in her forties.

LUCY stands with indecision. Then she bends down.

> LUCY
> (*whispering*)
>
> Diana . . . Diana . . .

Diana's eyes open, first with no recognition. Then:

> LUCY
>
> Hi.

DIANA
Lucy, Lucy!
(*Embraces her.*)
We were waiting for you to call.

LUCY
I got a cab.

DIANA
(*jumps up, takes* LUCY)
Come on in—
(*Entering the house, calling to an upper window:*)
Ian, wake up! Lucy's here.

They disappear inside. A man's head appears in the upstairs window,
IAN GRAYSON, an artist in his midfifties, sees no one below.

INTERIOR. KITCHEN. DAY.
The kitchen is abundant with fruit and vegetables. The furniture is
clearly handmade, colorfully decorated. As DIANA prepares some vegetables, LUCY notices a swallow in a nest above her head. She inspects
pictures on the sideboard: an erotic Indian miniature, a photograph
of four generations of Englishwomen, and a small bust by IAN of a
bare-breasted girl.

DIANA
Tell me about your father . . . and his new wife.

LUCY
They're trying to have another baby.

DIANA
I had Daisy when I was forty. I cannot get over how
grown-up you look!

> LUCY
>
> I hope so—after four years.

LUCY gazes at a photograph of two young men. Close-up of one. This is NICCOLÒ DONATI with Diana's son, CHRISTOPHER.

> LUCY
>
> Is Christopher here?

> DIANA
>
> He was supposed to turn up yesterday—for my birthday. But Christopher's still floating somewhere around Turkey with his friend Niccolò.

> LUCY
>
> Niccolò Donati?

> DIANA
>
> Do you remember him?

> LUCY
> (*nods*)
>
> Yeah . . .

IAN GRAYSON, awakened from his nap, enters the kitchen. He's a handsome Irishman, robust, with a slightly awkward manner.

> IAN
>
> Lucy, welcome!
> (*Steps across the kitchen to kiss her.*)
> Welcome, welcome.

> LUCY
>
> Hi! How are you?

EXTERIOR. COTTAGE LAWN. DAY.

LUCY follows IAN, who carries her bags across a lawn. LUCY looks around at the terra-cotta figures scattered about in the grass.

>   LUCY
> I remember this exactly, just from one week!

>   IAN
>   (*pointing to some boxes*)
> My bees . . . If you don't bother them, they won't bother you.

They arrive at a stone cottage facing the pergola.

>   IAN
> See, we fixed up the old hay barn—it only took us twenty years. When we first came there was nothing, no water, no heat. We spent every penny we had just to buy the place . . .

>   LUCY
> Why'd you move here?

>   IAN
> For work. There's a great tradition of art in these hills.

INTERIOR. COTTAGE. DAY.

IAN and LUCY pass an open doorway to a room with medicine on the table, an unmade bed.

INTERIOR. LUCY'S ROOM. DAY.

IAN opens one shuttered window. LUCY pulls at the shade of another window—much larger—which opens to a wide view.

                              IAN
In the room next door you've got Alex Parish. An old
friend of ours . . . He knew your mother, too. He's been
very sick. Distressing for everyone.

                              LUCY
The writer?

LUCY looks around the large loft-like room. IAN observes her.

                              IAN
I hope you're patient, because I fumble along a bit.
You'll help me? . . .

                              LUCY
How?

                              IAN
Let me look at you.

                              LUCY
Not all the time, I hope.

                              IAN
You won't even be aware . . .
                    (*He moves to leave.*)
So. Get settled, take a swim. We eat at sunset, but come
up before.

IAN exits.

LUCY fishes through a duffel bag. She takes out a small knapsack. Inside is her journal. Out of an envelope she removes a faded Polaroid.

(Close-up: LUCY with a young man at the edge of the water with a
stone pillar.) She slips the snapshot under her shirt, over her heart.

LUCY faces the large window. On the next hill is a villa. She stares at it, knowing it.

She hears a noise outside the window. Below is a thin man in an armchair, grimacing in pain.

ALEX PARISH is an ailing English playwright in his late forties. He's bent forward, and spit slips from his mouth. He has aimed it. Close-up of spit falling, landing on an ant in the dirt.

A tornado noisily crosses the sky above the Tuscan valley.

His arm reaches up to adjust the cord of an I.V.

EXTERIOR. VILLA GRAYSON. SUNSET.
LUCY takes a puff of a cigarette. She's wearing a large shirt, with a one-piece bathing suit underneath.

As she walks along the portico, a slipper lands at her feet. She looks up and sees on the balcony an elderly man wearing a white suit and Panama hat, the man who'd been sleeping in the garden. M. GUILLAUME is an art dealer in his eighties.

> LUCY
> Is this your slipper?

> M. GUILLAUME
> I suppose so . . . Do I know you?

> LUCY
> I'm Lucy.

> M. GUILLAUME
> I am Guillaume. *Enchanté* . . . Here for a visit?

LUCY

Ian's doing my portrait. It's really just an excuse for my
father to send me to Italy as a present.

M. GUILLAUME
(*distracted*)

But where is Signor Bruno? I have a dream to tell him.

M. GUILLAUME disappears in the shade of the balcony.

LUCY
(*throws the slipper up onto the balcony*)

Hey! Your slipper!

M. GUILLAUME

Oh, *merci mademoiselle! Merci . . .*

LUCY

I'm going for a swim . . . Bye.

M. GUILLAUME

Merci.

INTERIOR. IAN'S STUDIO. SUNSET.

IAN, looking out the window at LUCY.

EXTERIOR. POOL. SUNSET.

At the end of a long vineyard LUCY arrives at the pool. She sees a young
naked woman lying asleep with a towel draped over her. LUCY removes
her shirt. She walks down the pool steps and slips quietly underwater.
Her mouth and nose gently break the water's surface like a trout. She
goes back under and swims down to pick up a piece of jewelry, an
earring.

Lucy's hand reaching for the feet of a statue on the side of the pool, her slick head following.

> MIRANDA
> (*offscreen*)
> Jesus, I thought you were drowning. I was wondering whether I was going to have to haul you out or not.

MIRANDA is Diana's pretty twenty-four-year-old daughter from an early marriage, a designer. When she lifts her head we see she's wearing bracelets, rings, etc.

> LUCY
> You Miranda?

> MIRANDA
> You were here before, weren't you?

> LUCY
> Four years ago. Your brother was here. Not you.

> MIRANDA
> I don't really live here. But we come every year for Mummy's birthday. To console her. Christopher's so distracted he couldn't quite find his way out of Turkey.

> LUCY
> With Niccolò?

> MIRANDA
> You know Niccolò?

> LUCY
> From last time.

MIRANDA

You don't smoke by any miracle, do you? Richard freaks
out when I smoke.

LUCY

Not really. . . . When are they coming back?

MIRANDA

Who?

LUCY

Your brother.

MIRANDA

Who knows? They said—
                    (*looking away*)
Richard.

RICHARD REED, an American lawyer in his late thirties with standard
good looks and an ingratiating manner, appears in jogging clothes.

RICHARD

Hi, babe!

MIRANDA

This is—you know . . . Harmon . . . Mummy's friend's
daughter . . .

LUCY

Lucy.

MIRANDA

Right—Lucy.

RICHARD
(*taking off his shirt*)

God, Sarah Harmon's daughter? Your mother was a great poet! Richard Reed—
    (*Shakes hands.*)
Really, really honored to meet you!

LUCY
It's my mother, not me.

RICHARD
Your mother made me want to be a poet once.
    (*Undoing his sneakers.*)
I think it would be great just to sit around all day and express yourself.

MIRANDA
Richard, I didn't know you wrote poetry.

RICHARD
Never did. Don't have a creative bone in my body.
    (*To* LUCY:)
But I became an entertainment lawyer so I can be around creative people—like Miranda.

LUCY looks at MIRANDA.

MIRANDA
    (*self-deprecating*)
I design jewelry. I apprentice with this real asshole in New York, but he's a genius!

LUCY
Is this yours?
    (*Hands her the earring.*)

MIRANDA
    (*throwing it back in the pool*)

Yes, but that's old shit.
                    (*To* RICHARD:)
You going in?

                    RICHARD
How is it in there, Lucy?

                    LUCY
Quiet as a tomb.

RICHARD stumbles stepping out of his underwear. Shot of RICHARD, naked, diving in. LUCY pulls out of the water.

INTERIOR. DINING ROOM. NIGHT.

NOEMI, M. GUILLAUME, IAN, and RICHARD are at the table. LUCY and DIANA carry food from the kitchen with MARIA. MIRANDA is on the phone.

                    MIRANDA
What? No, I'm losing your voice . . . You sound like you're at the bottom of the sea. You have to speak up. I can't hear you.

LUCY trying to listen to Miranda's conversation.

                    NOEMI
Listen to this: "*Cara Noemi, Ci sono due uomini nella mia vita. Uno è capace di appagarmi come non credevo fosse possibile ma si comporta come se io non esistessi. L'altro è affettuoso, ma niente sesso. Dimotra il suo amore per me ululando davanti alla finestra. Sono lacerata tra i due. Cosa devo fare?—L'Indecisa.*"

["Dear Noemi, There are two men in my life. One is able to please me like I never believed possible but he acts as if I don't exist. The other is affectionate, but no sex. He shows his love for me by howling in front of my window. I'm torn between the two. What should I do?—Undecided."]

Everyone laughs and starts to eat. MIRANDA sits down beside RICHARD and gives him a kiss.

IAN
Who was on the phone?
(MIRANDA *and* RICHARD *continue to kiss.*)
Miranda, who was on the phone?

MIRANDA
Christopher.

DIANA
What did he say?

MIRANDA
They're not coming back.

DIANA
What, never?

MIRANDA
I don't know, they missed a connection or something—I couldn't hear.

Shot of Lucy's face, drinking wine.

M. GUILLAUME
Those naughty boys. I bet they're being very naughty.

MIRANDA
(*to* RICHARD)
I'm sure they've gone beyond naughty by now.

INTERIOR. STUDIO. NIGHT.
In the background movement of household after dinner. NOEMI is typing in the living room; MIRANDA and RICHARD are dancing in the kitchen to Billie Holiday; DIANA and LUCY are bent over a chest.

DIANA
Noemi writes a "Lonely Hearts" column called "*Ditelo a Noemi*"—"Tell Noemi." It has quite a following!

DIANA looks through a chest and brings out a white dress.

LUCY
I have a picture of Mum in this dress.

DIANA
She said after she got married she was going to be fat and happy and had no more use for it. Of course, she never gained an ounce.

DIANA
Try it on. You can wear it to the Donatis' party. They give a lovely one every summer.

DIANA looks at her.

DIANA
You know, you could be Sarah twenty years ago, coming to help fix up this place.

LUCY
(*skeptical*)
She helped you fix up this place?

DIANA
Well, with a lot of hash breaks.
I think it's a bit long. Here, I'll pin it up.

LUCY climbs on the chest. DIANA pins it.

DIANA
Your mother needed to risk things. That kind of person ends up hurting others, I think, without meaning to.

LUCY
I don't think she really noticed.

DIANA
Oh, Lucy, she did. She hurt herself the most.
(*Pause.*)
But I admired the recklessness in her. It's so . . . not me!
I thought it brave. I couldn't live like that. I'm not the type. And neither is Ian. You know, I think we've been faithful to each other for twenty years. Can you believe that?

LUCY
Yes.

DIANA
Most people can't.

INTERIOR. LUCY'S ROOM. MAGIC HOUR.

LUCY at the window, a joint in her mouth, writes in a worn journal. Overlapping handwriting. She looks straight into the camera, then writes.

> I have her secret deep within
> For years I've had to hide.
> I've brought the clues and now I'm here
> To bring the truth outside.

She rips out the poem and burns it in the candle's flame, then lets go of it in the air.

INTERIOR. IAN AND DIANA'S BEDROOM. NIGHT.

DIANA moving around. IAN is in bed with a book.

> IAN
>
> Very strange, that father of hers . . . He never cared for my work. He hated the portrait I did of Sarah. Why does he suddenly want Lucy to come here?

> DIANA
>
> Maybe it was Lucy who wanted to come. Now she's stranded with us old fogies . . .

> IAN
>
> Speak for yourself.

> DIANA
>
> I'm sure she'd rather be out chasing boys around on a beach somewhere.

> IAN
>
> She seemed rather serious to me.

DIANA

Or being chased.
                         (*Putting on a robe.*)
At nineteen it's all about boys. You know, I caught her
looking at a picture of Christopher.

IAN

Christopher?

DIANA
                         (*picks up a sewing basket*)
Why not? She's nineteen—
                         (*Goes to the door.*)

IAN

Not sleepy?

DIANA

No. Not at all. I've got to finish Daisy's dress. I must
switch off all the lights. I'll try not to wake you up when
I come in.

IAN

Come here.
                         (DIANA *does.*)
Goodnight kiss?
   (*She kisses him on the forehead, then turns to go.*)
That all?
         (*She turns back and kisses his mouth.*)

IAN

You were nineteen once, I suppose, weren't you?

DIANA
                         (*at the door*)
I suppose I must have been.

INTERIOR. LUCY'S ROOM. NIGHT.
LUCY smoking a joint in bed. She lies down, then abruptly turns over.
Through the wall, she hears ALEX coughing.

LUCY rolls over again, puts a pillow between her knees. She restlessly
turns, unable to sleep. Close-up of her feet, one foot stroking the other.
Close-up of her face, tears covering her cheeks. With two fingers she
wipes the tears, then her hand moves down her body. On her face,
signs of transport. She begins to breathe more heavily.

Suddenly, the door creaks open.

> LUCY
> Yes.

A face appears in the doorway.

> ALEX
> Excuse me, but you wouldn't happen to have any more
> of that exotic brand of cigarette I smell?

Lucy's face.

EXTERIOR. COTTAGE. NIGHT.
ALEX is leaning on the pergola post. LUCY hands him a joint. They
smoke.

> ALEX
> It's not my best play—

> LUCY
> I really liked it.

> ALEX
> —but it's the one they'll remember me for.

He hands LUCY the joint. She smokes it through her cupped hand.

ALEX

I'm not contagious, you know.

LUCY

I always smoke this way—with other people.

ALEX

One doctor gave me three months. One said a week or
two, depending. According to a third, I should be dead
as we speak. . . . I tend to think of the first doctor as
being the best.

LUCY

It's terrible.

ALEX

You're not one of those moralistic young people, are
you?

LUCY

What do you mean?

ALEX

I mean sex. Do you disapprove of sex?

LUCY

No.

ALEX

Nothing's more transporting, I seem to remember.
Except, perhaps, good grass.

LUCY

I wouldn't know, I haven't really had it that much.

ALEX

Grass?

LUCY

No, sex.

ALEX

You mean, you've never slept with anyone?
                    (LUCY *shakes her head.*)
A beautiful girl like you?

LUCY

No.

ALEX

Well. That's a pretty good secret.

LUCY

Do you remember her wearing a pair of green sandals?

ALEX

I don't think so. She might have done—she wore wonderful clothes. She was the best-dressed poet, writing
transporting little verses in between fashion shoots. Why
have you never wanted to sleep with anyone?

LUCY

It's not that I never wanted to sleep with anyone . . .

They both laugh, stoned.

ALEX

Come on. It's not as if I'll know for long.

LUCY
(disturbed, softening)
There was this one guy I really liked. I met him in the
summer when I was fifteen. He was the first person I
really kissed.

ALEX
Come on, come on . . .

LUCY
Well, we wrote each other for a while. There was this
one letter about him having an animal prowling through
his heart. I had memorized the whole thing.
(Pause.)
Anyway, after a while he just stopped.

ALEX
And then your mum died, and everything stopped.

LUCY
Her death has nothing to do with it. It's easier to stay
alone.

ALEX
Lucy, Lucy, Lucy. You can't have decided that at your
age.

LUCY
I haven't decided.

ALEX
You're in need of a ravisher.

LUCY
I'm waiting.

ALEX

Lucy, Lucy, Lucy.

LUCY

Would you stop saying that!

ALEX

You're scared. What is it you're scared of?
There's something else.
                    (*Studies her face.*)
I can see . . . you seem to be . . .

LUCY

Stoned. I'm going to bed.
                    (*She starts to leave.*)

ALEX

Don't forget this.

He gives her back the lighter, takes her wrist, smells the back of her
hand, lets it go.

ALEX

Sweet dreams.

In the distance is DIANA sitting on the terrace near the house, watching them, but unable to hear.

EXTERIOR. TERRACE. MORNING.

NOEMI and DIANA are setting the table for breakfast with MARIA, the
housekeeper. NOEMI and MARIA go back into the house. ALEX crosses
the lawn using a cane.

DIANA

Well, look who's up and about.

ALEX

I had a great night!

DIANA

You met Lucy.

ALEX

She's irresistible. I'm mad about her.

DIANA

Now, what's that smile about?

ALEX

What smile?

DIANA

Come on, tell.

ALEX

There's nothing to say, I mean, we just talked.

DIANA

What did she tell you?

ALEX

I have a feeling not as much as she might have done.

DIANA

Oh, come on!

ALEX

No, no, no. You can't keep a secret.

DIANA

Course I can!

ALEX

Really?

DIANA

Yes, really. Lately, I've been learning how. I've been practicing.

NOEMI
(*coming out with a breakfast tray*)
What's going on?

ALEX

Nothing's going on.

DIANA

Noemi, what would you tell your readers about a man who dangles a secret in front of you?

ALEX

I wasn't dangling!

DIANA

Yes you were!

ALEX

No, I wasn't!

NOEMI

He wants to tell it. "*Ditelo a Noemi.*"

INTERIOR. LUCY'S ROOM. MORNING.
Alarm wakes LUCY. She sits up in bed.

EXTERIOR. TERRACE. MORNING. LATER.

As LUCY approaches the terrace the chatter dies down: sudden quiet.
DIANA, NOEMI, ALEX, RICHARD, and MIRANDA are at breakfast. M.
GUILLAUME waters the plants around the pergola. An empty place is
set for LUCY.

> LUCY
>
> Sorry, my time's all screwed up.

They look at her. She sits down and we see each person looking at
her in a peculiar way. They all know; she remains unaware.

> DIANA
>
> Here—rub a little tomato on your bread. It's very
> Tuscan.

> MIRANDA
>
> We're going to have to find Lucy some friends, so she
> won't get bored with us old people.

> NOEMI
>
> Are we that old already?

Richard's cellular phone rings. He answers it, getting up.

> RICHARD
> (*leaving the table*)
> Hi, yah. What time is it there?

> MIRANDA
>
> How about Filippo Castellini? He's cute.

LUCY glances at ALEX, who avoids her look.

> NOEMI
>
> Terrible flirt.

ALEX
Noemi, would you pass me some sugar?

MIRANDA
What about Harry Fenimore-Jones?

ALEX
(*to* LUCY)
You take sugar?

DIANA
O.K., Miranda.

NOEMI
Too perverse for an American girl!

MIRANDA
Carter Clay! Carter Clay would love Lucy!

DIANA
Basta! Lasciatela in pace. È appena arrivata . . .
[Enough! Leave her alone. She's just arrived . . .]

LUCY
(*eating a huge piece of bread*)
I feel like a classified ad.

The sound of a bulldozer is heard in the distance.

ALEX
(*desperate to change the subject*)
You see what we have to put up with? Do you hear that?
You might as well be in downtown Manhattan.
(*Stands up, followed by the others.*)

RICHARD is talking on his cellular phone on the lawn, as the group
leaves the table.

RICHARD
(*As the group crosses the lawn.*)
Listen, gotta go.

The group follows ALEX to look at construction beginning on the next hill. RICHARD joins them.

RICHARD
What is that?

NOEMI
È un ripetitore.
[It's a repeater.]

ALEX
They're building a TV mast.

DIANA
For brainwashing the Italian electorate.

MIRANDA
You don't like it because it messes up your view!

M. GUILLAUME
(*stepping forward*)
Signor Bruno a été forcé de vendre son champ!
[Mr. Bruno was forced to sell his field!]
     (*spraying water in the direction of the bulldozers*)
Salauds! Ordures! Testa di cazzo!
[You bastard! You slime! You dickhead!]

ALL TOGETHER
Bravo! Bravissimo! Get 'em! More! More! More!

DAISY and IAN appear. DAISY, Diana and Ian's daughter, aged eight, runs toward her mother. She has an intent, penetrating air.

DIANA

Daisy!

RICHARD

Hi, Daisy! *Come stai?*

DIANA

My little piglet, how was Camilla's?

DAISY

Abbiamo visto Il mago di Oz!
[We saw *The Wizard of Oz!*]

DIANA

Again?

RICHARD
(*trying to make friends*)

Hi Daisy!

DAISY regards him with suspicion, and looks past him to LUCY.

DIANA

You remember Lucy? Last time she was here you were
only four.

DAISY approaches LUCY, frowning, then points to her bracelet.

DAISY

What's that?

LUCY

It's called a scarab. See? It's like a beetle. It's good luck!

IAN
(*reading the paper*)
There's a general strike tomorrow. I think I won't be here for lunch.

DIANA
But the shutters, Ian! You promised you'd paint the shutters.

DAISY
(*to* LUCY)
Want to see something?

LUCY
Sure.

DAISY
Come on. *Vieni—Mamma, tu resta qui, ce la porto io!* [Come on. Come—Mom, you stay here, I'll take her myself!]

LUCY and DAISY leave down the hill.

ALEX
Well, I thank you for being so fucking helpful. My God, I can't trust any of you!

DIANA
Miranda, you wouldn't stop . . .

MIRANDA
Me? It wasn't only me!

IAN
What?

ALEX
(*ignoring him*)
She's searching for something, with those long hands she can barely control and that curiosity and a little frightened. It reminded me so much of myself, somehow.

ALEX turns back toward the cottage.

EXTERIOR. LAKE. DAY.
The stone steps leading into the water are the same as in Lucy's Polaroid. LUCY and DAISY arrive running.

LUCY
You know, I kissed a boy here once.

DAISY
Did you touch tongues?

LUCY
Uh-huh.

DAISY
Miranda likes to kiss boys. She always kisses Richard and before that she kissed Matthew and Gianni . . . and Niccolò and David . . .

LUCY
She used to kiss Niccolò?

DAISY
At the fireworks!

INTERIOR. KITCHEN. AFTER DINNER.
The group is cleaning up. IAN carries glasses. MIRANDA and RICHARD fold a tablecloth. NOEMI puts bread away. M. GUILLAUME corks a bottle. LUCY carries in glasses, and speaks to DIANA as she washes dishes.

> LUCY
> Do you know a man named Carlo Lisca?

> DIANA
> Yes. He lives near Gaiole. Why, do you know him?

> LUCY
> Mummy used to get letters from him. What's he like?

> DIANA
> He's a very good war correspondent, but I think seeing so much death, blood, and horror made him a little peculiar. I'll ask him over. You can meet him.

> LUCY
> Do you remember her being in love with a man here?

> DIANA
> You mean Carlo?

> LUCY
> Well, I don't know, there was this thing that she wrote . . .

> DIANA
> Really, what did she write?

> IAN
> (*interrupting, from the doorway*)
> Lucy, I think the time has come.

LUCY turns. DIANA watches her follow IAN out.

> DIANA
> (*to* LUCY)
> Off you go!
> (*To* NOEMI:)
> He's gone to the studio. You know, he hasn't worked
> at night for years.

> NOEMI
> But there's a virgin in the house!

DIANA laughs.

INTERIOR. IAN'S STUDIO. NIGHT

Nudes tacked to the wall, discarded drawings on the floor. LUCY is
unsuccessful at staying still. IAN sketches. When he looks up she's in
a different position.

> LUCY
> It's cool in here.
> (*Pause.*)
> My father never came here.

> IAN
> Some people don't like to leave their country. I never
> met your father, you know.

> LUCY
> He's small. I'm five inches taller.

> IAN
> Really?

(*Crumbling a page, irritated.*)
Maybe if you concentrate on that . . . horse's leg, it
might be easier for you to stay still. Now I see where
you're different from your mother! You have a sort of
joy in your eyes.

LUCY
(*trying to keep still*)
Do you ever eat olive leaves?

IAN
Olive leaves? They're inedible, disgusting. Why d'you
ask?

LUCY
Just asking.
(*Pause*)
I can feel the night behind me.

IAN
Then you can see why we love it here. One thing, I do
miss though: The Gravediggers. . . .
(*Pause.*)
Best pub in Dublin. I think we've done enough for to-
night. You've been very good!

LUCY stands up. She kisses him goodnight.

EXTERIOR. HOUSE. NIGHT.
It is dark. LUCY walks back to the cottage. In the portico, through an
open door, she hears the sounds of RICHARD and MIRANDA making
love.

RICHARD
(*offscreen*)
That feels good. Oh my God. That's good. I'm your
daddy baby. Hmm.

MIRANDA
(*offscreen*)
Yes, yes, yes . . .

LUCY leans against the wall in awe. She slips to the ground, listening.

RICHARD
(*offscreen*)
Oh my God!

MIRANDA
(*offscreen*)
No, no, no.
(*Pause.*)
Yes, yes, yes.

LUCY, laughing a little, knocks over a rake. The sounds inside reach a
crescendo.

MIRANDA
(*offscreen*)
What was that?

LUCY flattens herself against the wall as RICHARD and MIRANDA appear in the door looking out.

RICHARD
(*whispering*)
Where is he going?

M. GUILLAUME appears, walking by in his pajamas, holding his slip-
pers with his left hand.

MIRANDA
Sshh. Don't wake him. You're never supposed to disturb sleepwalkers.

LUCY presses herself back in the shadows as M. GUILLAUME passes very close to her, staring ahead.

EXTERIOR. GRAYSON DRIVEWAY. TEATIME.
A car drives up. The hand of the passenger is familiar, with the same Middle Eastern bracelet worn by the MAN WITH CAMERA. The hand points at a yellow Deux Chevaux parked by Ian's studio.

CARLO
Guarda chi c'è! Noemi.
[Look who's here! Noemi.]

MICHELE
Noemi? "Ditelo a Noemi"?
[Noemi? "Tell Noemi"?]

CARLO
E già.
[That's right.]

CARLO LISCA is a journalist in his fifties. He and his son MICHELE, twenty-six, get out of a Saab. CARLO is a small man, his son much taller. They cross the courtyard.

EXTERIOR. TERRACE. TEATIME.

DIANA
(*whispering to* MIRANDA)
Here's the Marquis de Saab!

The Liscas cross the pergola. NOEMI comes out from the kitchen.

> CARLO
> (*embracing* NOEMI)
> *Che bella sorpresa! Conosci mio figlio? Michele... Noemi.*
> [What a beautiful surprise! Do you know my son?
> Michele . . . Noemi.]

> NOEMI
> (*shaking Michele's hand*)
> *Ciao. No, non ci conosciamo.*
> [Hi. No, we don't know each other.]

CARLO moves toward the terrace to greet the others. MICHELE and NOEMI remain together for a moment. In the background, LUCY and DAISY are playing on the lawn, with RICHARD doing his best to touch LUCY.

> MICHELE
> *Veramente, ci siamo visti una volta a Roma.*
> [Actually, we met each other once in Rome.]

> NOEMI
> *Ma sì, davvero?*
> [Oh yes, is that right?]

CARLO and MICHELE greet DIANA, MIRANDA, M. GUILLAUME, and IAN.

LUCY, running on the lawn, glances with interest at CARLO.

EXTERIOR. LAWN. TEATIME.
IAN and CARLO walk off toward the cottage. NOEMI and MICHELE are talking in the background, under a tree.

CARLO
(*recognizing* LUCY *as the girl on the train*)
Is that Sarah's daughter?

IAN
Yes, Lucy.

NOEMI and MICHELE talking apart.

NOEMI
Mi confondi con un'altra. Non mi sono mai vestita di viola.
[You're confusing me with someone else. I never wear
purple.]

MICHELE
*No, me lo ricordo benissimo. Aveva delle spalline e si vedeva
tutta la tua schiena nuda.*
[No, I remember perfectly. It had shoulder straps and
you could see all of your bare back.]

NOEMI
*Ma sai che, è vero—me lo aveva prestato un'amica. Non
posso credere che ti ricordi di una cosa simile.*
[You know what, you're right—it was borrowed from
a friend. I can't believe you remember such a thing.]

MIRANDA, from the terrace, shouts to RICHARD, still playing on the
lawn with LUCY and DAISY.

MIRANDA
Richard! Sweetheart. We're all going for a swim.

IAN and CARLO come upon Ian's group of sitting statues, near the
cottage.

On the lawn, RICHARD tackles LUCY.

She struggles with him, trying to push him off. He persists.

LUCY
(*suddenly impatient*)

Stop it!

CARLO looks toward the lawn at LUCY and slips on his sunglasses to hide.

MIRANDA
(*suddenly smashing a plate*)

Richard! Are you coming or not?

EXTERIOR. PORTICO. TEATIME.

The group walks down the driveway toward the pool. Among them are NOEMI and MICHELE.

NOEMI

Ce l'hai la ragazza a Roma? L'amore della tua vita?
[Do you have a girlfriend in Rome? The love of your life?]

MICHELE

Macchè!
[Come on!]

CARLO hangs back, walks off to a lemon grove, looking at a winding staircase going nowhere.

EXTERIOR. LEMON GROVE. TEATIME.

LUCY

You Carlo?

CARLO

Yes, I . . .

(*Lowers his sunglasses.*)

You're Lucy.

They start moving around the staircase. CARLO has a dark, menacing quality. She studies him.

LUCY

My mother used to mark a star on her calendar every time she got a letter from you.

CARLO

I was very fond of your mother. We had many jokes together. She appeared as this elegant woman, but she loved to act vulgar.

LUCY

That's not what I remember. I remember her sitting awake all night in the dark smoking cigarettes and listening to jazz records.

CARLO

Everyone has dark moods.

LUCY

Do you?

CARLO

Only when I'm away from war. Around war I am as light as a soufflé.

LUCY

Have you ever killed a viper?

> CARLO
>
> Of course, I grew up in the country.

He removes a strand of hair caught in Lucy's mouth.

> LUCY
>
> Did you ever meet my father?

> CARLO
>
> No. It's not what you think.
>   (*Awkward pause.*)
> We had only one night together. That's all.

> LUCY
>
> Only one night?

> CARLO
>
> We were friends . . .

> ALEX
>   (*offscreen*)
>
> Lucy!

ALEX appears outside Ian's studio.

> CARLO
>   (*walking off*)
>
> See you later.

ALEX joins LUCY.

> ALEX
>
> No, no, no . . . I don't think he's the one for you—not
> for my Lucy in the Sky!

LUCY
(*convincing herself*)
Actually, I like him.

ALEX
You do?

LUCY
There's something familiar about him.

ALEX
My illusions shattered. Come on, let us slowly bring up
the rear like Turgenev's poor Rakitin . . .

They walk off together.

EXTERIOR. POOL. TEATIME.
LUCY and ALEX arrive within sight of the pool.

ALEX
Oh, God! No . . . I can't bear it.

They look. Everyone is either swimming or sitting on the side of the
pool. They are all naked.

LUCY
What?

ALEX
(*turning away*)
It's so—unnatural.

He turns his back. LUCY keeps looking toward the pool, and over-
hears DIANA and CARLO talking. They do not see her.

CARLO
I felt I was being interviewed.

DIANA
She's curious about you. Can you imagine Sarah being
a virgin at nineteen?

CARLO
It's this generation. They're terrified of disease.

LUCY turns around and hurries back down the road, passing ALEX
without looking at him.

INTERIOR. LUCY'S ROOM. TEATIME.
LUCY pulls out her duffel bag from under the bed. Throws in clothes.

INTERIOR. STUDY. EARLY EVENING.
LUCY, writing on a pad, on the phone. DAISY sits in her lap with a set
expression.

LUCY
Sì. To New York. *Domani* . . .
[Yes. To New York. Tomorrow . . .]
(*She holds.*)

DAISY
Non partire, dai—What about having Christopher as
your boyfriend?
[Don't go, come on—]

LUCY
Who told you that?

DAISY
That's what Mummy told Noemi.

LUCY
(*on the phone*)
Sì. Quando?
[Yes. When?]

Through the doorway behind LUCY a young man appears carrying a dusty knapsack.

CHRISTOPHER
(*in the doorway*)
Oh, hello . . .

LUCY turns to CHRISTOPHER FOX, Miranda's brother, a twenty-two-year-old English fellow with a happy-go-lucky, yet melancholy air.

DAISY
Christopher!

CHRISTOPHER
Crazy Daisy!

DAISY
Piglet!

CHRISTOPHER
Piglet.

DAISY runs into his arms. He puts a red flag on her shoulders.

CHRISTOPHER
Here, the Turkish flag.

(*To* LUCY:)
I remember you—Lucy! Did I interrupt you?

There is a voice behind CHRISTOPHER.

NICCOLÒ
(*to* CHRISTOPHER)
This is the last time I carry your bag . . .
(*To* DAISY:)
Ciao piglettina!
[Hi little piglet!]

DAISY

Ciao, Niccolò!
[Hi, Niccolò!]

LUCY looks over Christopher's shoulder to see NICCOLÒ DONATI, a handsome twenty-three-year-old, the man in Lucy's Polaroid. He is wearing a well-traveled Turkish shirt.

NICCOLÒ
(*not recognizing* LUCY)
Hello—

CHRISTOPHER
Don't tell me you've forgotten Lucy . . .

Niccolò's face remains indecisive.

LUCY
(*hanging up the phone*)
No. I couldn't get through.

CHRISTOPHER
Lucy Harmon.

NICCOLÒ
Oh, Lucy! Of course, it's you!

Behind him, OSVALDO appears in the doorway.

NICCOLÒ
Osvaldo, conosci Lucy?
[Osvaldo, do you know Lucy?]

OSVALDO
Yes, a bit.
(*Pause.*)
Andiamo?
[Shall we go?]

CHRISTOPHER
Come and have dinner tonight.

NICCOLÒ
Dovrei vedere mia madre—
[I should see my mother.]

CHRISTOPHER
Portala—I'll get Mum to call.
[Bring her . . .]

NICCOLÒ
(*to* LUCY)
So I'll see you very, very soon!

INTERIOR. LUCY'S ROOM. EARLY EVENING.
LUCY unpacks a few of her clothes with a happy air. She goes to the
window and watches the Donati pickup truck drive over the hill.

INTERIOR. DONATI PICKUP TRUCK. EARLY EVENING.
In Italian. OSVALDO is driving.

NICCOLÒ
*Sì, ci siamo scritti per un po', ma l'ho vista solo quella
settimana là. Era molto diversa . . . Era piccola.*
[Yes, we used to write for a while, but I only saw her
that one week. And she looked pretty different then . . .
She was younger.]

OSVALDO
*Mi ricordo che scriveva un sacco. Scriveva sopra delle
vecchie cartoline.*
[I remember she wrote a lot. She used to write on old
postcards.]

NICCOLÒ
Sempre a leggere la mia posta!
[There you go reading my mail again!]

NICCOLÒ starts punching OSVALDO playfully. OSVALDO tries to defend
himself and drive at the same time. They sing Turkish song imitations.

EXTERIOR. COTTAGE TERRACE. SUNSET.
DIANA is carrying Alex's dinner tray toward the cottage.

DIANA
Dinner time!

ALEX
(*sitting in a chair*)
Do you think she's still angry with me?

Through the cottage window, DIANA catches sight of LUCY in her room.

DIANA

Darling, I don't think she's giving you too much
thought.

ALEX stands to follow and they look in Lucy's window. DIANA pulls
him away.

Through the window, LUCY with a Walkman on, madly dancing by
herself. Courtney Love singing "Rock Star."

EXTERIOR. PERGOLA. EVENING.
Through the window and the doorway of the kitchen, LUCY watches
the guests arriving. The Donati brothers and their mother, CHIARELLA,
a slightly dramatic and wistful woman, are welcomed by DIANA, IAN,
and NOEMI.

DIANA

Ciao, Chiarella!

CHIARELLA

*Ogni volta che vengo qui è come se arrivassi su un'altro
pianeta. Veramente siete riusciti a creare un mondo
speciale, tutto vostro. Beati voi! Un giorno, per venire qui
ci vorrà anche il passaporto!*
[Every time I come here it's as if I've arrived on another
planet. You've really managed to create a special world,
all your own. You're blessed! Someday, to come here
you'll even need a passport!]
But where's Lucy? I want to see Lucy!

LUCY looking through a curtain in the kitchen. NICCOLÒ surprises her
from behind.

NICCOLÒ

So, Lucy Harmon . . . How long are you staying and

what do you think of Italy and when are you going to
come to our house and see how real Italians live and
change your life—forever?

LUCY
You didn't even recognize me.

NICCOLÒ
You! You didn't recognize me!

Behind them, MICHELE with NOEMI. He gives her a book.

MICHELE
Ecco il libro di cui ti avevo parlato.
[Here's the book I was telling you about.]

NOEMI
Adolphe, *di Benjamin Constant.*
[*Adolph,* by Benjamin Constant.]

MICHELE
Parla di ideali e d'amore.
[It's about love and ideals.]

NOEMI
Una favola, insomma.
[A fairy tale, in short.]

MICHELE
Tu leggilo.
[Read it.]

They go out together. MARIA remains in the kitchen preparing
dinner.

Liv Tyler as Lucy Harmon.
Copyright © 1996 Twentieth Century Fox. All rights reserved.

Bernardo Bertolucci and Liv Tyler.

(Top) Liv Tyler as Lucy Harmon and Roberto Zibetti as Niccolò Donati. (Bottom) Jason Flemyng as Gregory and Liv Tyler as Lucy Harmon.

Jeremy Irons as Alex Parrish and Liv Tyler as Lucy Harmon.
Copyright © 1996 Twentieth Century Fox. All rights reserved.

Bernardo Bertolucci behind the scenes.

(Top) Sinead Cusak as Diana Grayson. (Bottom) Ignazio Oliva as Osvaldo Donati.

(Top) Rachel Weisz as Miranda Fox. (Bottom) D. W. Moffett as
Richard Reed.

(Top) Joe Fiennes as Christopher Fox. (Bottom) Liv Tyler as Lucy Harmon.

Copyright © 1996 Twentieth Century Fox. All rights reserved.

EXTERIOR. PERGOLA. NIGHT.

Having coffee are DIANA, CHIARELLA, IAN, CARLO, M. GUILLAUME, and RICHARD.

> CARLO
>
> *In questo paese nessuno ascolta gli altri. Tutti a proclamare le proprie opinioni. . . . È diventato il paese dei monologhi.*
> [In this country no one listens to others. Everyone declares his own opinion. . . . It has become a country of monologues.]

> CHIARELLA
>
> *E' una critica, o un'autocritica?*
> [Is he a critic or an autocritic?]

> CARLO
>
> *Tutti e due.*
> [Both.]

RICHARD stands up and walks toward lanterns and chairs where the young people are.

EXTERIOR. UNDER THE TREES. NIGHT.

MIRANDA with a glass of wine is passing a joint. With her are LUCY, NICCOLÒ, CHRISTOPHER, MICHELE, NOEMI, and OSVALDO.

> MIRANDA
>
> I decided I had to get rid of it in the summer . . . before I went back to school.

> RICHARD
> (*arriving from the pergola*)
> Darling, are you speaking of life before me?

RICHARD crawls over and puts his head in Miranda's lap. She awkwardly puts the joint in his mouth. An ash falls and burns him.

> RICHARD
> (*jumping up*)
> Fuck! Shit on a stick. That's what pot's all about.
> (*Passes joint to* LUCY.)

> MIRANDA
> I ended up doing it with the same guy my best friend did it with. He was the local deflowerer.

> LUCY
> I wonder how we got on this subject.

> CHRISTOPHER
> Miranda, I remember that guy. He was repulsive.

> MIRANDA
> He was creepy, I must admit.

> CHRISTOPHER
> I don't remember mine at all. I was completely drunk.

> NOEMI
> (*to herself*)
> *Ma cosa ci faccio qui con i ragazzini?*
> [What am I doing here with the children?]
> (*to* MICHELE)
> *E tu, Michele?*
> [And you, Michele?]

> MICHELE
> I was in a car. It was snowing.

RICHARD
I was eleven, tripping with my baby-sitter.

They all laugh, stoned.

MIRANDA
(*pointedly*)
Lucy?

LUCY
(*loudly, having gotten drunk*)
What about falling in love? You're not even mentioning falling in love.

M. GUILLAUME appears behind them.

M. GUILLAUME
(*walking by*)
"*Il n'y a pas d'amour; il n'y a que des preuves d'amour.*"

NICCOLÒ
(*translating to* LUCY)
"There is not love; there's only proof of love."

NOEMI
What about you, Osvaldo?

OSVALDO
(*apart*)
I don't know which is more ridiculous—this conversation or the silly political one going on over there.

LUCY
(*suddenly weaving toward* NICCOLÒ)
What about you?

NICCOLÒ

Not me.

LUCY
(*getting closer*)

Not you what?

NICCOLÒ

Love is not a word I use.

LUCY

That's the saddest thing I've ever heard.

NICCOLÒ

I think I miss a lot of trouble that way.

LUCY
(*whispering close*)

I think I've missed a lot of you.
(*Her head slowly lowers. She begins throwing up
on his legs.*)

NICCOLÒ

Oh, God!

NICCOLÒ holds her forehead.

LUCY
(*drunkenly*)

No, I'm O.K. . . . I'm sorry—Niccolò, Niccolò . . .
You've been too far away.

Everyone is immobile, suppressing laughter.

INTERIOR. LUCY'S ROOM. DAY.

LUCY with wet hair writing in her journal in the bathtub. She looks into the camera. Overlapping handwriting:

I wait, I wait so patiently
I'm quiet as a cup
I hope you'll come and rattle me
Quick! Come wake me up.

She pushes the scrap of paper through the window behind her. The sound of Richard jogging by. LUCY goes under water.

LATER.

There's a knock on the door. LUCY wearing a large shirt

LUCY

Yah?

She opens the door to RICHARD wearing jogging clothes and sunglasses.

RICHARD

Hi. So I was wondering—
(*Comes in.*)
—if maybe I could bum a smoke.

LUCY

I thought you hated smoking.

RICHARD

Yes, well—don't tell Miranda. I guess I really have to quit, someday. So, I've never been down here.
(*Glances at the painted door.*)
Ha, so this is like the view—I get it.
I had a loft in New York, but I must say the bathroom wasn't completely exposed to the entire room.

(*Picks up her journal.*)
What have we here? So you do write?

LUCY takes the book from him, hands him a cigarette.

RICHARD
Sorry. What d'you write—your fantasies? I mean, you
do have fantasies, don't you?

LUCY
Everybody does.

RICHARD
There's an exercise actors do to explore their fantasies
and shed their inhibitions. Have you ever tried that?
Giving up control.

LUCY
(*watching* RICHARD *with suspicion*)
How?

RICHARD
Like, get on your knees.

LUCY
Right. On my knees.

RICHARD
No. I mean, I'll show you.

LUCY
(*considering*)
O.K., you go first.

RICHARD
O.K.

RICHARD gets on his knees and so does LUCY.

RICHARD
Now on all fours.

LUCY
(*suppressing laughter*)
You're kidding. . . .

RICHARD
No talking.

RICHARD gets on all fours. LUCY follows.

RICHARD
Now, go to the mirror—slowly.
(*close to the mirror*)
Open your mouth.
(LUCY *does*.)
Tongue out.

LUCY does, looking at RICHARD, whose tongue is out.

RICHARD
And lick . . .

LUCY looks at him as if he's crazy. She licks the mirror.

RICHARD
And lick. Just like a cat.

(*Licks mirror.*)
And lick. Good little kitty. Miaow . . . and lick. One
more time.
(*His tongue strays across the mirror toward her tongue.*
She laughs, pulling away.)
And now—

There's a sound at the door. MIRANDA enters.

                         MIRANDA
Lucy, I was just wondering— Oh. Richard! What's
going on here?

RICHARD scrambles up.

                         RICHARD
                     (*embarrassed*)
Sweetie, you know, we were just . . . Wait a second.
Wait!—

As they leave the room, LUCY sits against the wall and puts a hand
over her face, cringing, as if to say "what a disaster."

RICHARD and MIRANDA walk outside across the frame of the
window.

                         MIRANDA
Frankly, I don't know why you came. Either you're
jogging your ass off or have your ear glued to the bloody
phone. Plus, you reek of aftershave. What were you
doing in there?

                         RICHARD
Nothing.

MIRANDA

For Christ's sake. You're in there sniffing around her like a dog.

RICHARD

Miranda, I was explaining the Lee Strasberg acting technique.

MIRANDA
(*incredulous*)

No, I'm sorry.

LUCY closes the window as MIRANDA stalks across the lawn followed by RICHARD.

EXTERIOR. DONATI DRIVEWAY. AFTERNOON.
LUCY riding a bike. She slows down, then turns up a driveway. She enters the gate of Casa Donati.

EXTERIOR. DONATI COURTYARD. AFTERNOON.
LUCY crosses the courtyard and gets off her bike. She stops at the open front door and knocks looking around.

LUCY
(*softly*)

Niccolò? . . .

INTERIOR. DONATI HALLWAY. AFTERNOON.
LUCY walking through a hallway painted with frescoes.

SERVANT
(*off*)

Cerca qualcuno, signorina?
[Are you looking for someone, miss?]

A servant appears on the stairs.

LUCY

No, sì. Dov'è Niccolò?
[No, yes. Where's Niccolò?]

SERVANT

È fuori in giardino.
[He's outside in the garden.]

LUCY

Grazie.
[Thank you.]

EXTERIOR. COURTYARD. LATE AFTERNOON.

LUCY walks out into the garden. Down the pathway she sees Niccolò's figure near a tree. She tiptoes close, then discovers a couple kissing. The man is lifting the woman's skirt. It is NICCOLÒ.

EXTERIOR. ROAD AMONG VINEYARDS. LATE AFTERNOON.

OSVALDO walks through the vineyards, carrying a live rabbit. LUCY riding quickly, rattled.

OSVALDO
(*waving*)

Ciao, Lucy!

After going by, she skids and falls. OSVALDO runs to help her.

OSVALDO

Did you hurt yourself?

LUCY

No.

OSVALDO

Are you sure?

LUCY

Yes.

LUCY gets up and picks up the bike, which rolls a little. After a moment of struggle, she controls it, gets on with a scraped knee, and rides away. OSVALDO watches her go.

EXTERIOR. BOTTOM OF GRAYSON DRIVEWAY. LATE AFTERNOON.

LUCY riding her bike among the vineyards. A man wearing a uniform is peering under the hood of a car. He calls to LUCY. She slows down.

LIEUTENANT

Scusi—
[Excuse me—]
            (*Following her.*)
Sa dove posso trovare un telefono?
[Do you know where I can find a telephone?]

LUCY points to the Grayson villa in the distance.

EXTERIOR. UNDER THE TREES. EARLY EVENING.

From the balcony, M. GUILLAUME looks down with curiosity, toward the LIEUTENANT talking on a cellular phone.

LIEUTENANT

*Va bene allora, mi raccommando: domattina, il più presto
possibile. Positivo.*
[All right then, please make sure: Tomorrow morning,
as soon as possible. Be sure.]

DIANA and NOEMI are painting furniture. MIRANDA is stringing beads.
DAISY is mending a bracelet. Tea is on the table. LUCY has left her
bike.

LIEUTENANT

They'll pick me up tomorrow morning, at dawn. Thank
you anyway.
(Turning to leave.)

LUCY

No—

MIRANDA

No, stay—

DIANA

Well, but you can't just go and sit at the bottom of the
drive!

The four women stir and flutter around flirtatiously.

MIRANDA

Would you like some tea? You in the highway patrol?

LIEUTENANT

I'm in the army.

DIANA
(handing him a cup)
You must try some honey. It's from our own bees—

MIRANDA
Some biscuits?

DIANA
What's your rank?

LIEUTENANT
Lieutenant. Thank you.

NOEMI
Ma come [lo] parla bene l'inglese, signor tenente!
[But how well you speak English, Mr. Lieutenant!]

LIEUTENANT
Grazie.
[Thank you.]

The LIEUTENANT sits down stiffly. DAISY carries her small chair around to sit near him.

EXTERIOR. COTTAGE. EARLY EVENING.
LUCY, limping slightly, passes ALEX, who's hooked up to the I.V. asleep in a chair outside. He holds a cigarette with a long ash near his face. Trying not to wake him, LUCY leans forward and removes it. As she tiptoes toward her room, his eyes blink open.

ALEX
Don't be cross with me.

LUCY steps back.

ALEX
I am sorry. Please forgive me.

LUCY notices his posture is weaker.

LUCY
We're all going to a pizzeria for dinner—if you want to
come.

ALEX
I think I'll pass on that.
(*Noticing her knee:*)
What have you done?

LUCY
It's just a scratch. It's O.K.

ALEX
It's terrible. . . . Wait. I'll do something.

ALEX unhooks the I.V. from the center of his chest, stands up.

INTERIOR. ALEX'S ROOM. EARLY EVENING.
Alex tends to her scrape.

ALEX
You know, Lucy, you mustn't let it get to you.

LUCY
What?

ALEX
Us. We don't mean any harm. It's just that up here on
this hill the only thing we have to talk about is each
other.

LUCY
(*as he pours alcohol on the scratch*)
Ouch!

EXTERIOR. LUCY'S ROOM. MOMENTS LATER.

LUCY brushes her hair. ALEX is by the door.

> ALEX
>
> Your coming here has done me so much good. Better than any drugs. You're a walking I.V.

LUCY appears in the doorway, wearing a different dress.

> ALEX
>
> Do you know French?

> LUCY
>
> *Comme ci, comme ça.*
> [So-so.]

> ALEX
>
> *"L'incroyable frivolité des mourants"*. . . You must allow me a little frivolity.

LUCY kisses him on the cheek.

INTERIOR. PIZZERIA. EVENING.

The Grayson household plus MICHELE and the LIEUTENANT sit at a long table.

> IAN
>
> *Ma tenente, come mai da queste parti?*
> [Lieutenant, what brings you around here?]

> LIEUTENANT
>
> English please. I'm here for work, but not something I'm permitted to discuss.

RICHARD

Top secret?

NOEMI
(*suppressing laughter*)

Top secret?

MICHELE

Missione ostacolata da gomma a terra.
[Mission thwarted by a flat tire.]

OSVALDO, NICCOLÒ, and a girl in a peacock-blue dress enter. LUCY glares at her.

CHRISTOPHER
(*standing up, enthusiastically*)

Venite a sedervi con noi!
[Come sit with us!]

NICCOLÒ

No, avete già cominciato. Questa è Gabriella.
[No, you've already started. This is Gabriella.]

THE GROUP

Hi! *Ciao!*

NICCOLÒ

No, no. Ci mettiamo di là.
[No, no. We'll sit over there.]

M. GUILLAUME
(*suddenly*)

Jamais de la vie!
[Never in my life!]

Everyone looks toward the head of the table. After a moment, they continue eating.

                              DIANA
Someone take more bruschetta—Lieutenant?

                            LIEUTENANT
Thank you, no. Garlic gives me gas.

They all laugh, except LUCY, who is staring at NICCOLÒ sitting close to GABRIELLA.

                         M. GUILLAUME
Get this shit off the table!
                            (*Pause.*)
I can't piss in that shit-pile.

                               IAN
Here we go . . .

                            LIEUTENANT
Have I said something wrong?

                              DIANA
He's a very well-known art dealer, a legend, really, but sometimes he has these episodes . . .
                      (*To* M. GUILLAUME:)
Guy, on rentre?
[Guy, shall we go?]

                         M. GUILLAUME
When you visit, please fuck your mother!

DIANA
(*standing behind him and putting her hands
on his head*)
Tu es fatigué. Up we go.
[You're tired . . .]

M. GUILLAUME
(*smiling to her*)
Tu es une jolie slut!
[You're a pretty slut!]
(*looking straight into the camera*)
Je vous aimais tous, mais quand vous étiez vivants.
[I loved you all, but when you were alive.]

DAISY
(*apart to* LUCY, *knowledgeably*)
M. Guillaume is very theatrical.

CHRISTOPHER
Are the angels talking again, Mr. G.?

LIEUTENANT
(*coming forward*)
Perhaps I could—

IAN
I think we can manage it.

M. GUILLAUME
(*catching sight of the* LIEUTENANT)
I'm sorry, *mon ami.* I haven't a car for you.

LIEUTENANT
*Ça va. Vous savez, je préfère marcher. Vous voulez venir
avec moi?*

[That's quite all right. You see, I prefer walking. Would you join me?]

M. GUILLAUME
(*gets up, smiling*)
Vous êtes très aimable.
[Most kind of you.]
(*Leaves on the Lieutenant's arm, followed by* IAN *and* DIANA.)
Bonsoir, good-bye.

EVERYBODY
(*improvised*)
Bonsoir. Ciao. Bonne nuit. Good-bye. *Ciao.*

DIANA
See you all at home.

M. GUILLAUME
Je n'ai pas fini ma pizza.
[I have not finished my pizza.]

LUCY glances toward the table where the Donatis sit.

EXTERIOR. LOWER LAWN. NEXT DAY.
IAN is drawing LUCY in the shade of a tree. She looks at his strong arms and hands, studying him. When he looks up, her eyes look away.

She is looking more than he. He pauses from drawing. DAISY appears.

DAISY
Lucy, wanna play?

IAN
Daisy, Lucy's helping Daddy with his work.

DAISY leaves and runs toward MIRANDA. She is sitting on a rock in the
middle of the lawn, observing RICHARD under the pergola.

> DAISY
> Miranda, wanna play?

> MIRANDA
> I'm not in the mood for playing with piglets . . .

> DAISY
> *Uffa! Nessuno vuol giocare.* I'm bored. Nobody wants to
> play!
> [Uh! No one wants to play. . . .]

DAISY approaches RICHARD.

> RICHARD
> (*on the phone in German*)
> *Nein, nein, hör doch zu, ich weiss was wir machen mussen.*
> *Wir haben schon das amerikanische Erlebnis mit dieser*
> *Strandscheisse—*

RICHARD puts his hand over Daisy's mouth. She bites him.

DAISY goes and sits next to CHRISTOPHER, who's at his computer. At
the end of the table, NOEMI is sorting piles of letters.

IAN whispers something to LUCY. Then he goes back to his stool and
resumes his work.

From a distance, viewed from the terrace. Wanting to appear sophis-
ticated and trusting, LUCY slips the top of her dress down, baring her
breast. IAN draws.

EXTERIOR. PERGOLA. DAY.

MIRANDA, unhappy, smoking, walks over to CHRISTOPHER at his computer. She picks up a scrap of paper in the grass and hands it to him.

RICHARD, on his portable phone, watches LUCY, glances around to see if anyone else notices.

CHRISTOPHER looks at LUCY and types in:
Hi, my name is Lucy. I'm nineteen. I'm a virgin.

Inside a telephone rings. NOEMI knocks over a chair, hurrying in.

INTERIOR. STUDY. DAY.
NOEMI on the telephone.

>   NOEMI
>   (*coolly*)
> *Sì, Michele , , , No so se verrò stasera . . . Si, l'ho finito.*
> *Però è molto deprimente . . . No, scusa: è un libro*
> *veramente molto deprimente!*
> [Yes, Michele . . . I don't know if I'll come this evening
> . . . Yes, I finished it. But it is very depressing . . . No,
> wait: it is a really very depressing book!]

EXTERIOR. LOWER LAWN. DAY.
M. GUILLAUME sits in the shade near LUCY and IAN, watching unabashedly. Nearby, DAISY hits a tree trunk with a switch.

>   DAISY
> Take that! And that! And that!

In the distance, the Donati pickup appears.

EXTERIOR. PORTICO. DAY.
NICCOLÒ and OSVALDO notice LUCY, topless, under the tree.

>   NICCOLÒ
> *Niente male.*
> [Not bad.]

OSVALDO shrugs.

> NICCOLÒ
> *Ah, non stai guardando?*
> [Oh, you're not looking?]

> OSVALDO
> *Una che non s'imbarrazza mai davanti a nulla non è*
> *attraente. Ma guardala, è di plastica.*
> [Someone who is never embarrassed by anything is not
> attractive. Look at her, she's plastic.]

> NICCOLÒ
> *Eh già, la butteresti fuori dal letto!*
> [Right, you'd kick her out of bed!]

> DIANA
> (*in the doorway*)
> *Ragazzi, è tutto pronto—bicchieri, piatti . . . Venite!*
> [Guys, it's all ready—glasses, plates . . . Come!]

> OSVALDO
> (*getting out of the car to follow her*)
> *Ciao*, Diana.

EXTERIOR. LOWER LAWN. DAY.

DAISY and M. GUILLAUME walk away together toward the cottage.

> IAN
> If I'm not ready now, I'll never be ready.
> (*Stands up.*)
> You are free.

IAN walks off. LUCY pulls up her dress and turns to see Niccolò watching her. She walks across the lawn.

EXTERIOR. ROAD BY THE PORTICO. DAY.
NICCOLÒ watches LUCY, then gets out of the car to follow her.

EXTERIOR. UNDER THE PERGOLA. DAY.
NICCOLÒ crosses the lawn. CHRISTOPHER, MIRANDA, and RICHARD watch him follow LUCY. Through the kitchen window, OSVALDO watches him too.

INTERIOR. STUDIO. DAY.
IAN stands in front of a dark mass. We hear the sound of a buzz saw. He begins sawing a block of wood.

EXTERIOR. OLIVE GROVE. DAY.
LUCY and NICCOLÒ wander among the trees.

> LUCY
> When did Gabriella leave?

> NICCOLÒ
> This morning. I asked her to.

> LUCY
> Why?

> NICCOLÒ
> I wanted to see you.
> (*Touches her.*)

Lucy.

LUCY looks around.

> LUCY
> So, this is an olive grove?

> NICCOLÒ
> Yes.

LUCY walks over to a tree, snaps off a leaf, and eats it.

> NICCOLÒ
> (*ignoring her odd behavior*)
> You looked very beautiful back there. I could not take
> my eyes away.
>   (*Slips the straps from her shoulders.*)
> Like this. I wanted to—

He kisses her shoulder. LUCY looks thoughtful.

> NICCOLÒ
> I need to kiss your mouth—
>   (*They kiss.*)
> After this long time . . .

They embrace. His hand moves over her ass and begins to lift her
dress. She takes his hand and pulls him to the ground. They hold
each other. He moves on top of her. NICCOLÒ continues to kiss her
and caress her.

> NICCOLÒ
> *Dio, Lucy. È così bello . . . Mi piace sentirti.*
> [God, Lucy. This is so lovely . . . I like to feel you.]

His hand slips into her crotch. She pushes him back a little.

>   LUCY
>   (*nervously*)
> Wait.

He hardly pauses.

>   NICCOLÒ
> Please, Lucy . . . I'm dying for you. I'm dying.

LUCY closes her eyes. He keeps caressing her. Suddenly her eyes open.

>   LUCY
> Not here. I can't. I can't.

She stiffens. NICCOLÒ ignores it and continues bearing down on her.

>   LUCY
>   (*suddenly panicked*)
> No! Stop! Stop!

She scrambles to her feet and runs away, distressed.

>   NICCOLÒ
> What is it?

NICCOLÒ watches her hurry toward the cottage.

INTERIOR. ALEX'S ROOM. DAY.
From his room, ALEX catches sight of LUCY arriving at the cottage and entering her room.

INTERIOR. LUCY'S ROOM. DAY.

LUCY comes in, distressed. She stands in the middle of the room. She touches herself where NICCOLÒ has touched her. She touches her mouth and goes to the mirror, crying. She looks at her face searchingly, in conflict with herself. She suddenly turns and pulls out the duffel bag from under the bed. She takes out the journal.

INTERIOR. ALEX'S ROOM. DAY.

LUCY appears in the doorway and pauses.

> ALEX
> (*not looking well*)
> What's the matter?

LUCY enters.

> LUCY
> (*holding her mother's diary*)
> This was my mother's, from right before she died. It's about me.

> LUCY
> (*starts reading*)
> "Where have they gone, the green sandals? I was not made to be a mother, I had too stricken a heart, so I wore green sandals to stay apart. Then one night a man stood in an olive grove. He beat a viper till it bled, then drew me down low. I went farther than he'd ever know. One night was all there was. He fed me an olive leaf, then broke the strap of my dress."
> (LUCY *becomes upset.*)

ALEX walks over to LUCY.

ALEX
(*joins her on the bed and keeps reading*)
"I kept on the green sandals. But I could not get off that
hill. Italy, where did you take me that night so black
and still? He took the green sandals from me. He had
an accent and a knife and somewhere even had a wife.
He took my face and tore my hips and planted in their
place something new and strange and near to love . . . I
thought I had nothing left. But you came later, curved
and new. Forgive me, I did not have the means for catching when I got, poor Lucy, you."

Pause.

LUCY
It's my real father.

ALEX
It would seem so.

LUCY
(*suddenly*)
It's not you, is it?

ALEX
Can you picture me beating a viper? I don't even know
what a viper looks like.

LUCY
I thought it was Carlo Lisca—

ALEX
Really?

LUCY

But now I'm not sure. Maybe I should just forget about
it. I already have a father I love.
(*She gets up.*)

ALEX

No. I was never able to ask for the things that I needed.

Pause.

LUCY

Have you ever been in love?

ALEX

Lots of times.
(*Pause.*)
No.
(*Pause.*)
Just once.
(*His eyes close.*)

LUCY

Alex?
(*No answer.*)
Alex!

ALEX

Just feeling a bit . . . grotty today.

LUCY

Can I get you something?

She tries to hand him a cushion. He pushes it away.

ALEX

No. Don't fuss. I'll be all right in a minute. I'm just
feeling a bit rough, that's all.
(*Pause.*)
Don't give up. You'll find him. You won't disappoint
me.

INTERIOR. STUDIO. EVENING.
LUCY, dressed in the white dress, enters the studio quietly. She goes
to look under the cover and is interrupted by IAN, who is at the door.

IAN
(*surprising her*)
Don't you look nice!

LUCY

Can I see?

IAN
(*suddenly*)
No!
(*Steps toward her.*)
I mean, I never let anybody look until it's finished.

LUCY
(*uncertainly*)
Does it look like me?

IAN

It's not supposed to.

LUCY

It's not?

IAN

Course not. Didn't anyone ever tell you the artist always only depicts himself?

LUCY
(*laughing*)

Thanks a lot!

DIANA appears in the door.

DIANA
(*to* IAN)

Sure you don't want to come?

IAN

It's been the same for the last twenty years. Why should tonight be different?

DIANA
(*steps to* IAN)

And I thought life with you would be one long party!—
(*Stroking his cheek.*)
Not so.

DIANA and LUCY go out together. IAN watches them go.

EXTERIOR. DONATI DRIVEWAY. EVENING.
An alley of cypress trees. Distant music is playing. A spread-out procession of guests walk up toward the house, the Grayson household among them.

DIANA
(*beside* M. GUILLAUME)

This reminds me of dances I used to go to when I was a girl. Silly, isn't it, to feel homesick in such a magic place?

M. GUILLAUME
Beauty wounds the heart.

MIRANDA is walking with exasperation beside RICHARD. His phone rings inside his jacket.

MIRANDA
(*to* RICHARD)
I don't believe you have actually brought that thing!

NOEMI
(*to* LUCY)
Something surprising always happens every year at this party. You'll see, Lucy!

They enter the garden. Guests sitting on the grass, standing, kissing hello. CHIARELLA greets them. A small brass band is playing. They all wear billed caps.

EXTERIOR. DONATI GARDEN. EVENING.
LUCY glances at NICCOLÒ, who passes by sharing a slice of watermelon with a girl. Among the guests, LUCY spots CARLO LISCA. She approaches him, then sees him start a conversation with two women at a table.

MICHELE and NOEMI together. They reach for a glass of champagne passing on a tray. They stop near the band.

NOEMI
Ma perchè un libro che parla di un giovane che distrugge completamente una donna più vecchia di lui che lo ama?
[Why are you giving me a book about a young man who completely destroys an older woman who loves him?]

MICHELE
Il giovane non c'entra niente. Io m'identifico con lei!

[The young man doesn't mean anything to me. I identify with her!]

NOEMI
Come scusa, non c'è male.
[As an excuse, that's not bad.]

LUCY walks along the stage and sees OSVALDO in the band, playing a clarinet. The band stops playing. She claps.

INTERIOR. STUDIO. EVENING.
IAN is in his studio looking at the sculpture of LUCY.

EXTERIOR. DONATI HOUSE. EVENING.
Food is being passed around. The party is quite lively now. Suddenly, professional dancers run out of the gallery carrying torches through the garden. CHRISTOPHER follows one of them, entranced.

DIANA
(*to* M. GUILLAUME)
C'est très bon, ça. Tu veux? Délicieux . . .
[This is very good. You want some? Delicious . . .]

GROUP
Well, look at that! What is he doing? It's Christopher!

The dancer, still followed by CHRISTOPHER, passes by.

DIANA
(*to* CHRISTOPHER)
Sweetheart, is it what you want to do in life?

They run away.

> MIRANDA
> (*to* LUCY)
> Darling, let me do you a favor.
> (*Takes her hair down.*)
> That's better!

LUCY walks up to CARLO, who is eating. Beside him is NICCOLÒ with another girl.

> LUCY
> Do you want to dance?

> CARLO
> (*mid-bite*)
> Now?

> LUCY
> Now.

CARLO stands up. LUCY follows him, after having put her glass between NICCOLÒ and the girl.

INTERIOR. DONATI GALLERY. NIGHT.
CARLO enters the empty gallery, followed by LUCY. They start dancing together.

> LUCY
> Do you happen to remember where you were in August 1975?

> CARLO
> I try to forget. But that was after the fall of Saigon. Hard to forget the fall of Saigon.

LUCY
But after, did you come back to Italy?

CARLO
I don't think I ever came back.

Dancers from the group suddenly appear from the back of the gallery and pass by toward the exit with intriguing movements. A drunken woman, MARTA, weaves across the dance floor, heading for CARLO. She appears at Lucy's side.

MARTA
Ah, tu saresti quella nuova, eh?
[You the new one?]

LUCY
What?

MARTA
I'll show you what this bastard likes!

She squats down, nearly tipping over, pulls up her skirt, and pees.

CARLO tries to pull MARTA away, but LUCY grabs her at the last minute.

CARLO
(*amused, almost proud*)
Marta, ma che cazzo fai?
[Marta, what the fuck are you doing?]

LUCY finds herself helping MARTA up. The music changes. Blondie's "Heart of Glass." Dancers flood the dance floor.

EXTERIOR. DONATI GARDEN. NIGHT.
A shot of the full moon. On the stage, MICHELE is singing an aria from Mozart's *Don Giovanni* for NOEMI.

MICHELE

Deh vieni alla finestra
o mio tesoro
Deh vieni a consolar
il pianto mio
—se meglia vuoi dar
—non essere gioia mia crudel

NOEMI steps up to him and puts her hand over his mouth. She steps near the bushes, unzips her dress, and walks away. MICHELE rushes after her.

INTERIOR, DONATI BILLIARD ROOM. NIGHT.

LUCY stands in the doorway of a billiard room where people are shooting pool. Just inside the door is GREGORY, a well-built Englishman, quite pickled, sitting alone in an armchair. The party has thinned out but an air of enthusiastic dissipation remains.

GREGORY
You look as if you've lost something.

LUCY
(*uncertainly*)
I haven't lost anything.

GREGORY
Perhaps I can help you find it.

LUCY sees NICCOLÒ close to yet another girl.

LUCY
Do you have a cigarette?

GREGORY
Will a cigar do?

LUCY

Please.

GREGORY lights Lucy's cigar. M. GUILLAUME, followed by DIANA, MIRANDA, and RICHARD, leave the room. They all glance in Lucy's direction.

LUCY
(*to* GREGORY)
Do you ever get the feeling you're being watched?

GREGORY strangely nods, as he realizes one of the dancers is staring at him with her head upside down.

EXTERIOR. DONATI GARDEN. NIGHT.
OSVALDO sees LUCY and GREGORY walking out together. Suddenly, OSVALDO jumps out of a crowd, to catch up with LUCY.

OSVALDO
(*takes Lucy's wrist*)
Wait!

LUCY
(*surprised*)
Yah, why? . . .

OSVALDO
I wanted to ask you something. I'm coming to America and I wanted to ask you about it.

LUCY
(*looking up at Gregory*)
Yah. Maybe later, we could—

OSVALDO

When?

LUCY

Tomorrow.

OSVALDO

O.K. I'll come over tomorrow.

OSVALDO turns back to GREGORY, who is dancing drunkenly by himself.

OSVALDO

Are you sure he can drive?

GREGORY
(*suddenly serious again*)
Course I can drive.
(*Takes Lucy's arm.*)
Come.

LUCY and GREGORY walk away down the cypress alley.

LUCY
(*turning back*)
Thanks for the party.

INTERIOR. IAN'S STUDIO. NIGHT.
IAN with DIANA before him, in her evening dress. There is the noise of a car arriving. The car stops and LUCY and GREGORY get out.

EXTERIOR. DRIVEWAY. NIGHT.
LUCY notices DIANA looking out the studio window with IAN behind her. She pulls GREGORY over and embraces him dryly.

LUCY
(*whispers*)
Hug me . . . No kiss!

She leads him off. They walk drunkenly together along the terrace.

GREGORY
Absolutely no kissing, no! Because I am, above all, an Englishman and a gentleman—

LUCY glances up at Christopher's window. Beside him appears a dancer's silhouette. The sex of the dancer is not evident.

INTERIOR. IAN'S STUDIO. NIGHT.
IAN, dusty from work, with DIANA. Leaning against a sculpture, she pulls up her evening dress. They embrace.

INTERIOR. MIRANDA'S BEDROOM. NIGHT.
MIRANDA and RICHARD undressing. RICHARD in the doorway, watching LUCY.

EXTERIOR. UNDER THE PORTICO. NIGHT.
LUCY pulls GREGORY into a hug.

LUCY
(*whispers*)
Grab my ass.

GREGORY
(*whispers*)
No kissing. No kissing.

Then she stops him.

LUCY

Come on.

INTERIOR. MIRANDA'S ROOM. NIGHT.

RICHARD looking at LUCY.

RICHARD

(*to* MIRANDA)

Hey, babe. Come here for a second. Check that out.
Look at her.

(*Grabs her and kisses her. She pulls away.*)

I like it when you're mad!

He throws her onto the bed.

INTERIOR. ALEX'S ROOM. NIGHT.

ALEX, looking unwell, is nervously paging through books, looking
through bookshelves. He hears Lucy enter with someone.

INTERIOR. LUCY'S ROOM. NIGHT.

LUCY followed by GREGORY.

GREGORY

I know how it looks. They are wonderful, wonderful
friends, really. They just have this strange habit of dis-
appearing, which means, as usual, I've been completely
abandoned.

He sits heavily on the bed.

LUCY

I'll be right back.

GREGORY

Right.

(*Falls across the bed.*)

LUCY leaves. She stands in front of Alex's room. She wants to go in.

INTERIOR. ALEX'S ROOM. NIGHT.
ALEX puts his hat on, hearing her.

ALEX

Come in.

LUCY enters.

LUCY

Hi.

ALEX

Hi.

LUCY

So, I brought someone back.

ALEX

I heard. Who's the lucky fellow?

LUCY

A guy from the party.

ALEX

Italian?

LUCY

English, actually.

ALEX

Oh, English.

(*Pauses, wincing with pain.*)

Well, I'm proud to be close by such an auspicious
moment.

LUCY

What are you doing?

ALEX

(*feverish*)

I've lost something. And I think it might be one of the
best things I've ever written.

(*Pauses.*)

Of course, I would think that since I can't find it.

(*Long pause.*)

Go on. Off you go.

LUCY

'Kay . . . night.

She turns.

ALEX

(*muttering*)

Off you go.

LUCY

(*turning*)

What?

ALEX

Nothing.

LUCY leaves.

INTERIOR. LUCY'S ROOM. NIGHT.
LUCY wearing a big T-shirt. GREGORY is asleep on the bed. She leans forward, takes a pillow from behind him, then goes to the couch.

> GREGORY
> (*opening his eyes*)

Where are we?

> LUCY
> (*pulling a blanket over herself*)

Nowhere.

> GREGORY

What are you doing?

> LUCY

Going to sleep.

> GREGORY
> (*not moving*)

No. 'Course not. I will absolutely sleep there.
> (*staring up*)

Oh— Spinny head . . .

> LUCY

It's O.K.

> GREGORY

No. I absolutely insist.
> (*Passes out.*)

INTERIOR. CHRISTOPHER'S ROOM. NIGHT.
CHRISTOPHER with the dancer. The bed's legs scraping vigorously on the floor.

INTERIOR. IAN'S STUDIO. NIGHT.

IAN and DIANA are making love against a statue.

INTERIOR. MIRANDA'S ROOM. NIGHT.

MIRANDA and RICHARD thrashing around on the bed.

INTERIOR. LUCY'S ROOM. NIGHT.

LUCY, awake, staring up.

INTERIOR. OUTSIDE LUCY'S ROOM. MORNING.

GREGORY and LUCY leaving her room. She peeks inside Alex's door and sees him asleep. GREGORY tries to look.

> LUCY
>
> No!

LUCY leads him away.

INTERIOR. ALEX'S ROOM. MORNING.

ALEX in bed, looking awful, sees LUCY and GREGORY walking out.

INTERIOR. MIRANDA'S ROOM. MORNING.

MIRANDA is making jewelry at the table. RICHARD is getting dressed.

> RICHARD
>
> I don't know what you are complaining about. You've been getting what you want when you want it.

> MIRANDA
>
> So I'm supposed to be grateful. I can already picture

your next summer in Nantucket with some WASP
heiress.

                    RICHARD
Excuse me, have I misled you in some way? What hap-
pened to what you see is what you get?
                    (*Comes near her.*)
Come on. This isn't you. I know you.

                    MIRANDA
Tell that to your wife. Tell your wife how well you know
me.

RICHARD throws his bag on the bed. MIRANDA with tears in her eyes.

INTERIOR. ALEX'S ROOM. MORNING.
DIANA helps ALEX drink, holding his head in her hand.

                    DIANA
I'm going to call Dr. Signorelli.

                    ALEX
God, no. He smells like rotting meat.

                    DIANA
Alex, you need more help, darling.

                    ALEX
I'm all right.

                    DIANA
We can't do enough for you here.

ALEX
(*very weak*)
Lucy choose a good one?

DIANA
(*trying to smile*)
Well, she chose her first one.

ALEX
I am glad. Oh, God.
(*Squeezes her hand against the pain.*)
It's ludicrous, isn't it? About to snuff it . . . and still—

DIANA
Still chasing tail.
(*Pause.*)
That's how you are.

EXTERIOR. IAN 'S STUDIO. MORNING.
Miranda's car drives out of the driveway, revealing LUCY and GREGORY
next to car. They stand in front of each other, smiling awkwardly.

LUCY
So— Thank you.

GREGORY
Right.
(*Laughs.*)

GREGORY gives her a little knock on the cheek. He gets into his car,
then his head appears in the window.

GREGORY
Thank you . . . for what exactly?

LUCY
Nothing.

GREGORY
Right.

LUCY
Bye!

GREGORY drives down the driveway, and a car comes the other way—
Dr. Signorelli's car. LUCY follows it. IAN watches her.

EXTERIOR. BACK GARDEN. DAY.
From the pergola, LUCY watches DIANA walking up from the cottage
with DR. SIGNORELLI. She is fearful.

DIANA
Ha il terrore dell'ospedale.
[He's terrified of the hospital.]

DR. SIGNORELLI
*Solo lì lo possono aiutare. Ormai è solo questione di
allievargli il dolore, poverino.*
[Only there can they help him. Now it is only a ques-
tion of alleviating the pain, poor man.]
        (*Suddenly agitated, swatting the air.*)
Attenta! Un'ape!
[Watch out. A bee!]

INTERIOR. STUDIO. DAY.
IAN chiseling. DIANA enters.

She pauses.

She gets up and goes to him. They embrace.

DIANA
(*crying*)
He's got to go. He's got to go.

In the middle of a hug, she turns away, distressed. She leaves the studio.

EXTERIOR. COTTAGE. DAY.
ALEX carried on a stretcher by two ambulance drivers. DIANA and DAISY
beside him. On the lawn, IAN, NOEMI, MICHELE, CHRISTOPHER, and
M. GUILLAUME standing about, watching. LUCY is apart.

ALEX
(*to* IAN)
Oh, give me a ciggie, Ian?

IAN
For God's sake Alex, have you ever actually bought a
cigarette?

ALEX
Last time you bought a shirt!
(*Begins humming to himself.*)
Good-bye-ee, good-bye-ee . . .

NOEMI standing with MICHELE.

ALEX
(*To* DAISY, *very weak.*)
It's like being in a parade, isn't it?

M. GUILLAUME seems particularly moved by the sight. Everyone stands
loosely about as ALEX is loaded into the ambulance.

ALEX
If you could all see yourselves!

LUCY disturbed.

EXTERIOR. DRIVEWAY. DAY.
Outside the ambulance.

> LUCY
> (*whispers to* DIANA)
> I don't want to see him at the hospital.

> DIANA
> That's fine. You stay here. Say good-bye to him.

INTERIOR. AMBULANCE. DAY.
LUCY climbs into the ambulance with ALEX.

> ALEX
> (*weakly*)
> Let me see if you look different.

> LUCY
> (*hesitating*)
> I didn't really, you know—
> (*Stops.*)

> ALEX
> You musn't mind me. I've so enjoyed watching. All that
> beauty—aren't we lucky?

LUCY kisses him on the lips. She hands him a joint.

> LUCY
> Take it with you.

ALEX

There's my girl. I'll share it with the nurses.

LUCY
(*about to cry*)
See you.

She presses her face to his chest and gets out. DIANA climbs in next to ALEX. The doors shut.

INTERIOR. ALEX'S ROOM. AFTERNOON.
LUCY writing on the *Herald Tribune.* Overlapping handwriting. She looks into camera.

LUCY
(*writing*)

The die is cast
The dice are rolled
I feel like shit
You look like gold.

She tears the poem out and hides it inside a book. She slips it under Alex's pillow. At the window, she sits near Alex's tray.

Through the window, she sees Ian's statue of a mother with child.

EXTERIOR. WILDFLOWER FIELD. DAY.
LUCY picks wildflowers, making a bouquet.

INTERIOR. IAN'S STUDIO. EVENING.
LUCY enters the studio carrying a huge bunch of wildflowers. IAN is working.

LUCY
Do you remember where you were in August 1975?

IAN
(*looking up*)
We bought the house the spring of that year . . . So we
would have been here, I think.

IAN resumes his work.

LUCY
It's when I was conceived.

IAN is thoughtful.

LUCY
What?

IAN
Nothing.

LUCY
You looked like something . . .

IAN
No, I was just thinking . . .

LUCY
What?

IAN
I think that was when I did your mother's portrait.

They pause.

LUCY
(*puts down the flowers*)
That's what I thought.

IAN
I couldn't be sure. Diana'd remember— No, no, no.
Wait, actually she was in London then, sorting out
her divorce and the custody of the kids, so she'd be no
help to ask. It was one of the few times we've ever been
apart . . .

LUCY
No, I wouldn't ask her.
(*touching the flowers*)
These are for you.

LUCY breaks the spell, gesturing toward the sculpture.

LUCY
So am I done?

IAN
What? Oh . . . almost.

LUCY
Can I see now?

IAN
If I show it to you, it must be our secret.

LUCY
O.K.

IAN
You can keep a secret, can't you?

                                    LUCY
Yes.
                                  (*Pauses.*)
I learned from the master.

                                    IAN
How did you get to be such a lovely girl?

Ian puts his arm around her and they walk toward the sculpture. After
a pause, LUCY embraces him.

EXTERIOR. LEMON GROVE. DAY.
OSVALDO arriving at Villa Grayson. He glimpses LUCY leaving Ian's
studio and follows her.

EXTERIOR. AT THE BEEHIVES. DAY.
LUCY walking past the beehives. Suddenly her arms start hitting the
air, ducking from the bees. She covers her head. OSVALDO grabs her.

                                  OSVALDO
Come! Come with me.

EXTERIOR. SPRING. DAY.
There is a small spring in a hollow between the slant of the hills. LUCY
and OSVALDO are by the water. OSVALDO takes a handful of mud from
the edge of the water.

                                  OSVALDO
Where did they get you?

                                    LUCY
Here, and here.

She points to her upper arm, then to her neck.

> OSVALDO
> (*putting on mud*)
> This clay is good for you. You O.K.?

> LUCY
> I'm not dying.
> (*uncovering her upper chest, and pulling back her shirt*)
> And here.

OSVALDO looks, rapt and shy. He hesitates. It is too much for him.

> OSVALDO
> (*handing her the mud*)
> Here, you better.

He watches her smear it on. LUCY steps away, looks back at him.

> LUCY
> Come walk with me.

He follows her.

EXTERIOR. PATH ALONG DRIVEWAY. DAY.
LUCY and OSVALDO walking.

> LUCY
> So, you want to come to America?

> OSVALDO
> I can't stand it here anymore.

> LUCY
> But it's beautiful here.

Across the road, we see some hookers. A motorcycle stops.

EXTERIOR. HAY FIELD. DAY.
LUCY and OSVALDO walking in a field with huge rolls of hay. They
run down a hill. They appear walking up the opposite side.

> OSVALDO
>
> When I was little, I thought this was a paradise. Our
> house was at the center of the world. My parents had a
> lot of friends, important politicians bending down to
> kiss me. Then, two years ago, one night at dinner, some
> men came to the door and asked to speak to my father
> and they took him away. To jail.

> LUCY
>
> God, why?

> OSVALDO
>
> He was part of the whole mess—all the corruption and
> bribes.

> LUCY
>
> Where is he now?

> OSVALDO
>
> In Santo Domingo. Hiding in a new life.

EXTERIOR. ROAD. DAY.
LUCY and OSVALDO walking on a dusty road.

EXTERIOR. CYPRESSES CIRCLE. DAY.
LUCY follows OSVALDO along kind of a circle of cypresses.

OSVALDO
I wrote you once, you know.

LUCY
You did not.

OSVALDO
I didn't sign it, so you probably thought it was from Niccolò.

LUCY
What was it about?

OSVALDO
I don't know. How much I liked you. How I thought of you when I was in the woods.

LUCY
You wrote that letter? I loved that letter. You didn't write that letter. I don't believe it. That was my favorite letter. I knew it by heart.
(*He starts running away.*)
Hey, wait!

OSVALDO
"Dear Lucy, I'm sitting on top of a hill thinking of you, alone with my dog . . ."

EXTERIOR. VINEYARD. SUNSET.
LUCY and OSVALDO emerging from the vineyard.

OSVALDO
This is my tree.

They walk up together toward a giant tree on top of a hill.

EXTERIOR. UNDER THE TREE. SUNSET.
LUCY and OSVALDO sitting under the tree, facing the sunset.

> OSVALDO
>
> You must miss your mother.

> LUCY
> (*tears brimming*)
>
> I can't even picture her face.

She begins to cry. OSVALDO puts his arm around her. She cries harder against his chest. After a while she looks up at him.

> LUCY
> (*almost laughing*)
>
> Why are you crying?

> OSVALDO
> (*embarrassed*)
>
> Because I want to kiss you . . . and I'm not able.
> *Non ci riesco.*
> I can't.

LUCY looks at him. She kisses him.

INTERIOR. KITCHEN. EVENING.
DIANA and IAN.

> DIANA
>
> I want to leave.

> IAN
>
> What?

DIANA

Here.

IAN

Leave here?

DIANA

Yes. I want to go home.

IAN

This is home.

DIANA

Not really

IAN

This is where Daisy was born.

DIANA

It's not the same anymore. I don't want to die here. I want to die where I belong.

IAN

You're upset about Alex. Moving's not going to change that . . .

DIANA

I'm tired of taking care of other people. I want to go back. I want to go back to where it's gray and damp and the milk goes off. I feel . . . I'm not . . . this anymore.

IAN

We can't go back, Diana.

MIRANDA enters.

> MIRANDA
>
> I put Richard on the train to Pisa.

> DIANA
> (*turning*)
>
> Did you?

> MIRANDA
>
> I'd had it . . .

> DIANA
> (*going to her*)
>
> Darling, good for you.

> MIRANDA
>
> Do you think I was mad?

> DIANA
>
> No, we all have ones like that.

CHRISTOPHER enters.

> CHRISTOPHER
>
> Where is everybody?

> MIRANDA
>
> Gone.

M. GUILLAUME enters, followed by DAISY. NOEMI and MICHELE join them.

> M. GUILLAUME
>
> *Bonsoir.*

MICHELE

Ciao!

NOEMI

What's for dinner?

MICHELE

I'm starving.

They all sit at the table, while DIANA opens the fridge, thoughtful.

IAN

Chips?

DAISI
(*suddenly*)

Where's Lucy?

EXTERIOR. UNDER THE TREE. NIGHT.

A villa in the distance. A fire is burning.

LUCY lying on her back. OSVALDO pulls up her bra, kisses her, and touches her. His hand slips under her pants, gently trying to bring her to orgasm. She gasps and sighs. Her right hand reaches for his fly. Close-up of hands, moving under clothes in the firelight.

LUCY, flushed, holds OSVALDO. He kisses her and after a while gets on top of her. He tries to enter her. She winces and cries out. They both concentrate. He manages to enter her. Her face shows that it hurts. His face is in a kind of swoon.

As he moves she breathes heavily under him. He comes with a little cry and falls against her face. They are both panting. They look at each other. He hugs her tightly to him. She looks happy.

After a moment he shifts to move off of her.

LUCY
(*breathless*)
No.

(*She holds him to her.*)
Stay.

She looks at OSVALDO, then looks up, pleased with herself.

They fall asleep by the fire.

EXTERIOR. ROAD. DAWN.
LUCY and OSVALDO walking together. They stop at the driveway. There are leaves in Lucy's hair.

OSVALDO
I want to come with you.

LUCY
Now?

OSVALDO
No. To America.

LUCY
Then do.

They kiss and part. She watches him run down the vineyard.

OSVALDO
(*turning back*)
It was my first time too!

EXTERIOR. GRAYSON DRIVEWAY. EARLY MORNING.
LUCY turns and walks toward the villa, radiant.

8.7.96 Romans 11.00 (6.8°) 64611